Brian Wildsmith

GOAT'S TRAIL

Oxford University Press
Oxford Toronto Melbourne

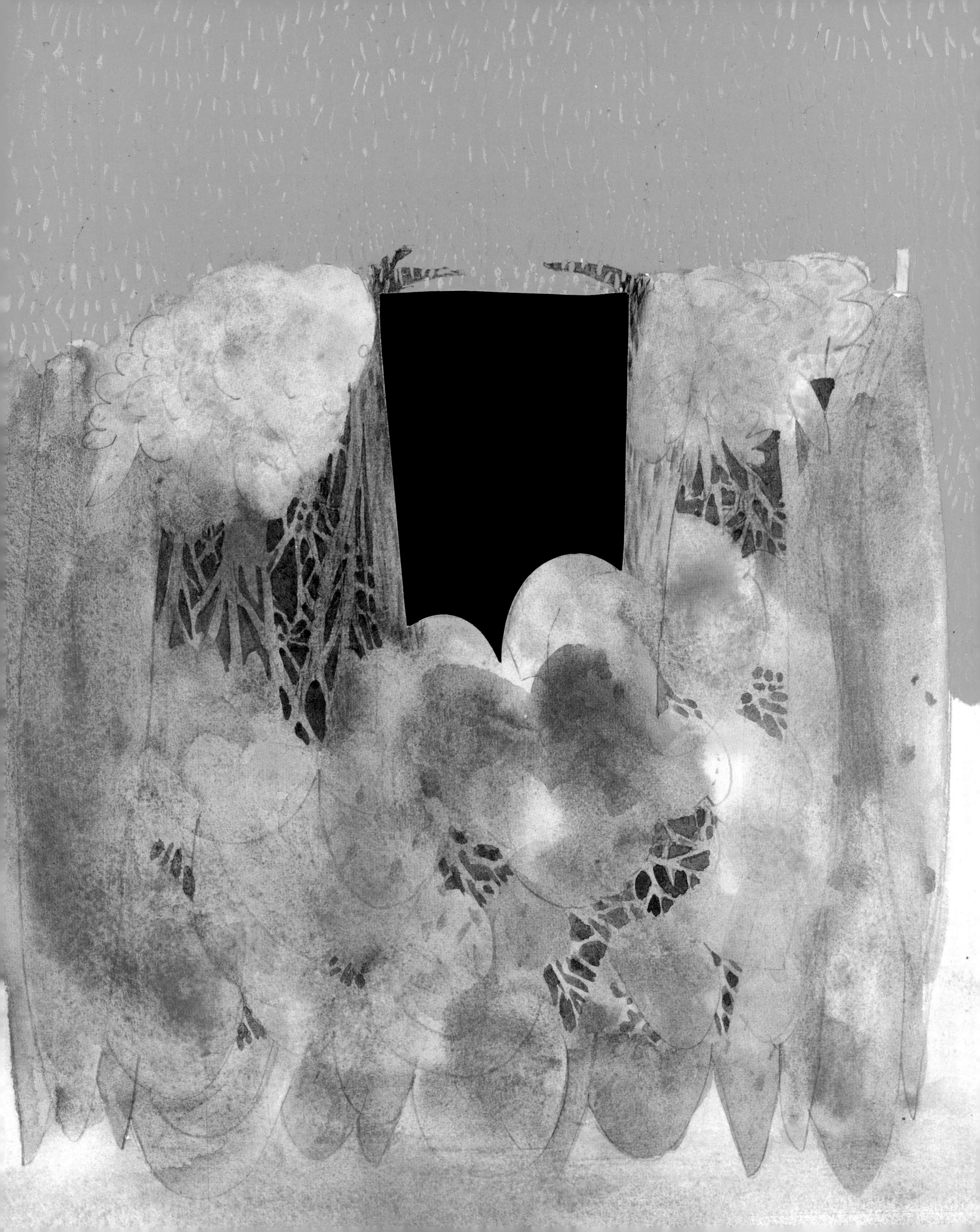

INDEX

There was once a wild goat who lived high in the mountains. 'It's nice to live so near the clouds,' he thought. 'But it's very dull and I get so lonely. All I ever hear are the buzz of the bees and the whistle of the wind.'

One day the wind carried new sounds up from a town in the valley.

DING DONG, VROOM VROOM, HONK HONK, UMP-PA-PA.

'That must be an exciting place,' he said to himself. 'I must go and take a look.' And off he went.

At the bottom of the mountain the goat met some sheep. 'I'm on my way to look at the town,' he told them. 'Why don't you come and follow me?'

The sheep looked at their shepherd who was fast asleep.

'BAA-BAA,' they said.

And off they went.

The sheep followed the goat towards the town.

'Listen,' said the goat. And the sheep perked up their ears to hear all the wonderful sounds that came from the town.

DING DONG, HONK HONK, VROOM VROOM, UMP-PA-PA, MOO MOO.

They approached the town and what did they see?

There was a cow, tied up to the wall.
'Poor little cow,' said the goat. 'I'll set you free.
Then you can come
and follow me.'

'MOO-MOO,' said the cow.

'BAA-BAA,' said the sheep.

'Follow me,' said the goat.

On they went, listening to the wonderful sounds all around them.

DING DONG, HONK HONK, VROOM VROOM, UMP-PA-PA.

But all of a sudden what did they see?

'GRUNT-GRUNT.'

There was a pig, tied on to a cart.

'Poor little pig,' said the goat. 'I'll set you free.
Then you can come and follow me.'

'GRUNT-GRUNT,' said the pig.

'MOO-MOO,' said the cow.

'BAA-BAA,' said the sheep.

'Follow me,' said the goat.

On they went, listening to the wonderful sounds of the town.

DING DONG, HONK HONK, VROOM VROOM, UMP-PA-PA.

But all of a sudden what did they see?

'HEE-HAW.'

There stood a donkey, hitched up to a cart.

'Poor little donkey,' said the goat. 'I'll set you free.

Then you can come and follow me.'

'HEE-HAW,' said the donkey.

They all climbed aboard and off they went.

They all rode into the centre of the town.

'HEE-HAW,' said the donkey, and he sat down right in the middle of the street.

VROOM VROOM, HONK HONK, BEEP BEEP.

'Get that donkey out of here!' shouted a policeman.

But the donkey refused to budge.

New sounds filled the air.

**BOOM-DE-BOOM, TA-RA TA-RA,
UMP-PA-PA, UMP-PA-PA.**

'Let's go and take a look,' said the goat. 'Follow me.'

The goat, the pig, the cow, and the sheep all jumped off the cart and ran down the street to the concert hall.

CRASH, SMASH, CLANG, BOOM.

'Get out of here!' yelled the leader of the band.

'GRUNT-GRUNT,' said the pig.

'MOO-MOO,' said the cow.

'BAA-BAA,' said the sheep.

'Follow me,' said the goat. And off they went.

They all ran out of the concert room into the street through an open doorway.

'A-B-C-D-E-F-G.'

'**HOORAY! HURRAH! YIPPEE!**' shouted the children.

'What is the meaning of all this noise?' said the teacher.

'The goat took my sheep,' said the shepherd.

'The goat took my cow,' said the farmer.

'The goat took my pig,' said the swineherd.

'**BAA-BAA,**' said the sheep.

'**MOO-MOO,**' said the cow.

'**GRUNT-GRUNT,**' said the pig.

'Get out of here!'
screamed the teacher.

'Follow me,' said the goat.

ABCDEFG
2+2=4
2+2+2=6
A
2+2+2+2=8

But this time, no one followed the goat.

They all went home . . .

. . . and so did the goat.

Oxford University Press, Walton Street, Oxford OX2 6DP
Oxford New York Toronto
Delhi Bombay Calcutta Madras Karachi
Kuala Lumpur Singapore Hong Kong Tokyo
Nairobi Dar es Salaam Cape Town
Melbourne Auckland

and associated companies in
Beirut Berlin Ibadan Nicosia

Oxford is a trade mark of Oxford University Press

First published 1986
ISBN 0 19 279834 0

British Library Cataloguing in Publication Data

Wildsmith, Brian
Goat's Trail
I. Title 823'. 914(J) PZ7

ISBN 0-19-279834-0

Set by Cotswold Graphics, Stroud, Gloucestershire
Printed in Hong Kong

For little Carla